VANILLA ICE CREAM

*For Vivian,
and for sparrows*

VANILLA
ICECREAM

Bob Graham

WALKER BOOKS
AND SUBSIDIARIES
LONDON • BOSTON • SYDNEY • AUCKLAND

The young sparrow rises from the dust.
He looks down at Annisha and Suhani.

He is young. He is curious ...

and bold.

Bold as a
truck-stop sparrow.

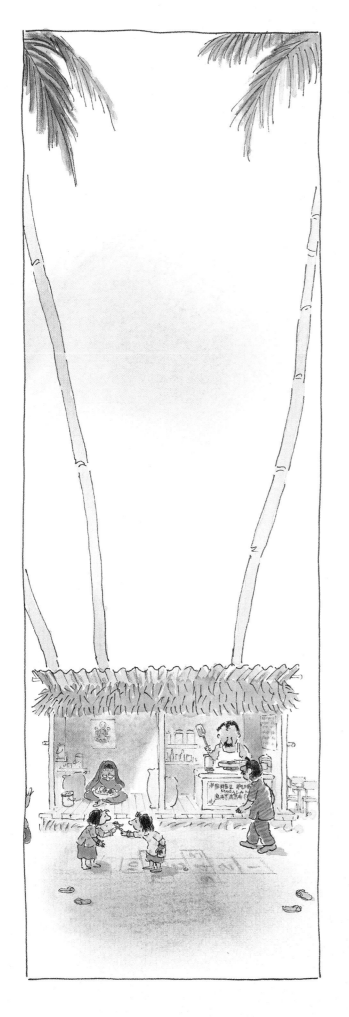

The sparrow is free to go
where he pleases.

And to eat ...

what he can find.

While the other birds
scuffle in the dust,

the sparrow leaves the truck stop for ever.

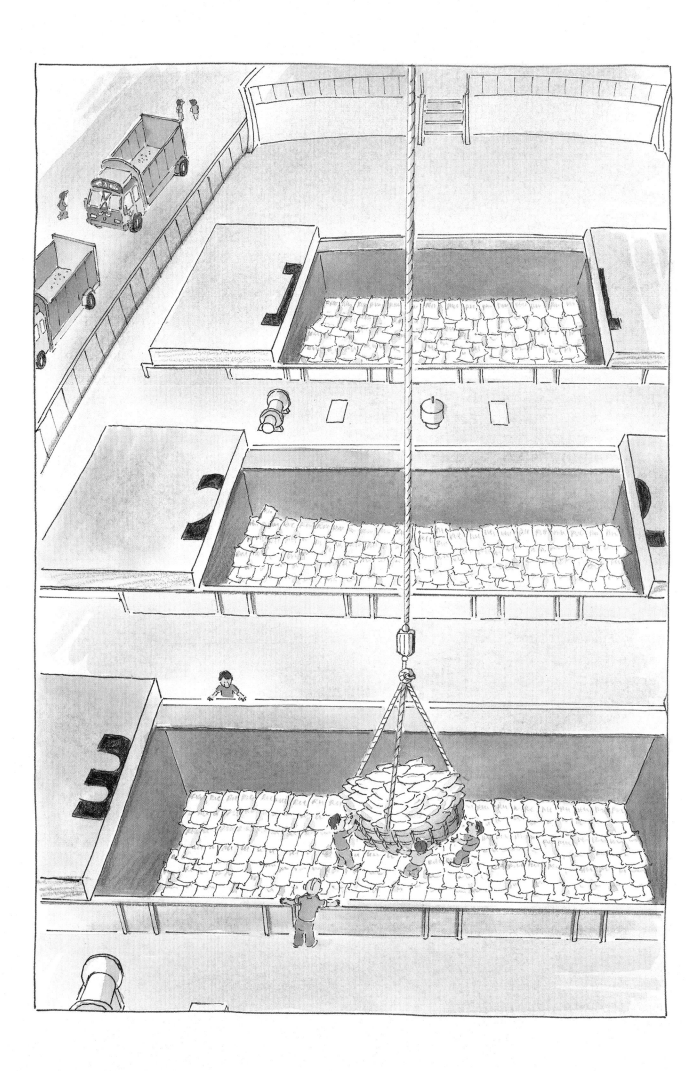

Like all wild birds,
he follows the food.

The truck-stop sparrow heads south.

He arrives into a bright new day.

Somewhere, somehow in this vast city he finds ...

Edie Irvine

and her grandma and grandad.

So it is ...

at the Café Botanica ...

in just one fleeting moment ...

Edie's life changes for ever.

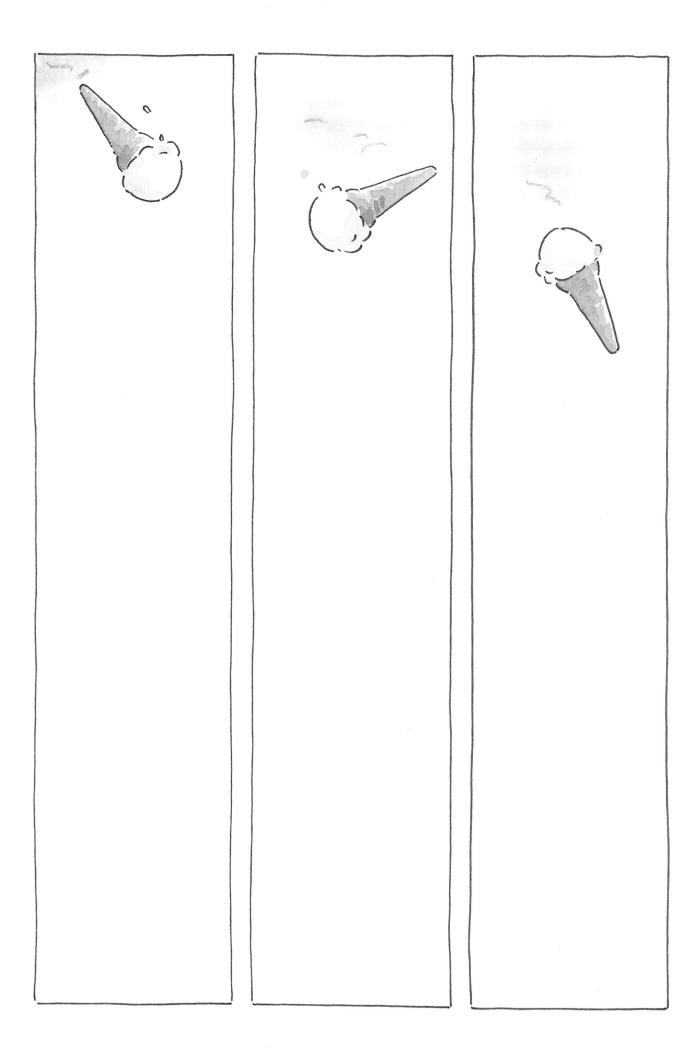

Edie Irvine, also young and curious,
for the very first time ...

discovers the taste of vanilla ice cream.

First published 2014 by Walker Books Ltd, 87 Vauxhall Walk, London SE11 5HJ ∗ 10 9 8 7 6 5 4 3 2 1
∗ © 2014 Blackbird Pty Ltd ∗ The right of Bob Graham to be identified as the author and illustrator of this
work has been asserted by him in accordance with the Copyright, Designs and Patents Act 1988 ∗ This book
has been typeset in Poliphilus ∗ Printed in China ∗ All rights reserved. No part of this book may be reproduced,
transmitted or stored in an information retrieval system in any form or by any means, graphic, electronic or
mechanical, including photocopying, taping and recording, without prior written permission from the
publisher. ∗ British Library Cataloguing in Publication Data: a catalogue record for this book is available
from the British Library ISBN 978-1-4063-5009-8 ∗ www.walker.co.uk

Amnesty International UK endorses *Vanilla Ice Cream* because it reminds us that we should all enjoy life, freedom and safety.
These are some of our human rights. Amnesty International protects people whose human rights have been taken away, and helps us
all to understand our human rights better. There are over three million members worldwide. If you would like to find out more about
us and human rights education, go to www.amnesty.org.uk or www.amnesty.org.au